Disney

Beauty and the BEAST

Friends Are Sweet

By Jennifer Liberts

Illustrated by Darrell Baker

A Random House PICTUREBACK® Shape Book

Hello, my name is Chip. I'm a teacup. My best friend is a very smart girl named Belle. We have lots of fun adventures together, but yesterday's takes the cake . . . well, the cupcake, actually!

It was Mama's birthday, and all her friends in the castle were busy planning a surprise party. Belle and I decided to make a sweet treat.

Belle turned toward the cupboards and said, "Who wants
to help make cupcakes for Mrs. Potts?"
Suddenly, the whole kitchen came alive! Everyone wanted
to help!

Belle and I mixed the ingredients together and poured the batter into the cupcake tin.

We put the cupcakes in the oven and asked Cogsworth,
the mantel clock, to let us know when they were done baking.

After the cupcakes cooled, Belle and I started decorating them. That's when I realized we'd forgotten something.

"Belle, we didn't ask Lumiere if he'd light the birthday candles," I said.

"Where *is* Lumiere?" asked Belle. "I haven't seen him all morning."

"Perhaps he's in the master's quarters," Cogsworth suggested.
"Yes," Belle said, "maybe Lumiere is lighting his fireplace."

Belle and I went to the master's quarters, but Lumiere wasn't there.

"Have you seen Lumiere?" I asked the Featherduster.

"No. Just a lot of dust bunnies," she said.

Next, Belle and I went to look in her bedroom. But we didn't find Lumiere there, either.

"We can't find Lumiere," I said to the Footstool. "Have you seen him?"

The Footstool wagged his tassels and ran to the door.
"I think he knows where Lumiere is!" cried Belle.

We followed the Footstool to the library.

"In here?" I asked the Footstool. He wagged his tassels some more and began sniffing around.

"I don't see him," Belle said sadly.

Suddenly, out of the corner of my eye, I saw some drops of wax on the floor.

"Look, Belle!" I called. "He was here! He was here!"

"If we follow the wax, we should find Lumiere," said Belle.

The drops of wax led down a cold, dark hallway. There were spiderwebs everywhere.

We continued to follow the wax. The hallway got darker and colder.

"I'm freezing! And it's so dark I can hardly see my handle," I whispered to Belle.

"Look," Belle said softly. "There's a light up ahead."

Belle was right!

"The light is coming from under that door!" I shouted. We ran toward it. Belle turned the doorknob and pulled, but she couldn't open the door.

"Lumiere?" called Belle. "Lumiere . . . are you in there?"

"Mademoiselle? Is that you?" shouted Lumiere from the other side of the door. "I've been stuck in this closet for hours. I was looking for decorations for the party when the wind slammed the door shut and locked me in!"

Belle rushed to close the window. Then the two of us pulled with all our might. The door finally popped open.

"Thank you, Monsieur Chip," said a relieved Lumiere. "Thank you, Mademoiselle."

"Now you can light Mama's birthday candles—that's your special job!" I said.

Everyone was happy to see Lumiere.

"You're just in time to light the candles," announced Cogsworth.
"Mrs. Potts is on her way!"

As Mama entered the room we all yelled, **"Surprise!**
Happy birthday!"
Mama was so excited she almost flipped her lid.

Mama thanked us for the cupcakes and Lumiere told her how Belle and I rescued him.

Belle gave me a kiss on the cheek. "I couldn't have found Lumiere without your help," she told me.

The cupcakes were sweet, but nothing's sweeter than my best friend, Belle!